For tigers everywhere
—P.B.

First published in the USA 2013 by Little, Brown and Company
First published in the UK 2013 by Macmillan Children's Books
This edition published in the UK 2014 by Macmillan Children's Books
an imprint of Pan Macmillan,
a division of Macmillan Publishers Ltd
20 New Wharf Road, London N1 9RR
Associated companies throughout the world
www.panmacmillan.com

ISBN: 978-1-4472-5328-0

3 5 7 9 8 6 4

A CIP catalogue record for this book is available from the British Library.

Printed in China

MR TIGER GOES WILD

peter brown

Macmillan Children's Books

Everyone was perfectly fine
with the way things were.

Everyone but Mr Tiger.

Mr Tiger was bored with always being so proper.

He wanted to loosen up.

He wanted to have fun.

He wanted to be . . . wild.

And then one day

Mr Tiger had

a very

wild idea.

He felt better already.

Mr Tiger became wilder and wilder each day.

His friends did not know what to think.

And then Mr Tiger

went a little too far.

His friends had lost their patience.

So Mr Tiger ran away . . .

. . . into the wilderness . . .

. . . where he went completely wild!

But Mr Tiger was lonely.

He missed his friends.
He missed the city.
He missed his home.

So Mr Tiger decided to return . . .

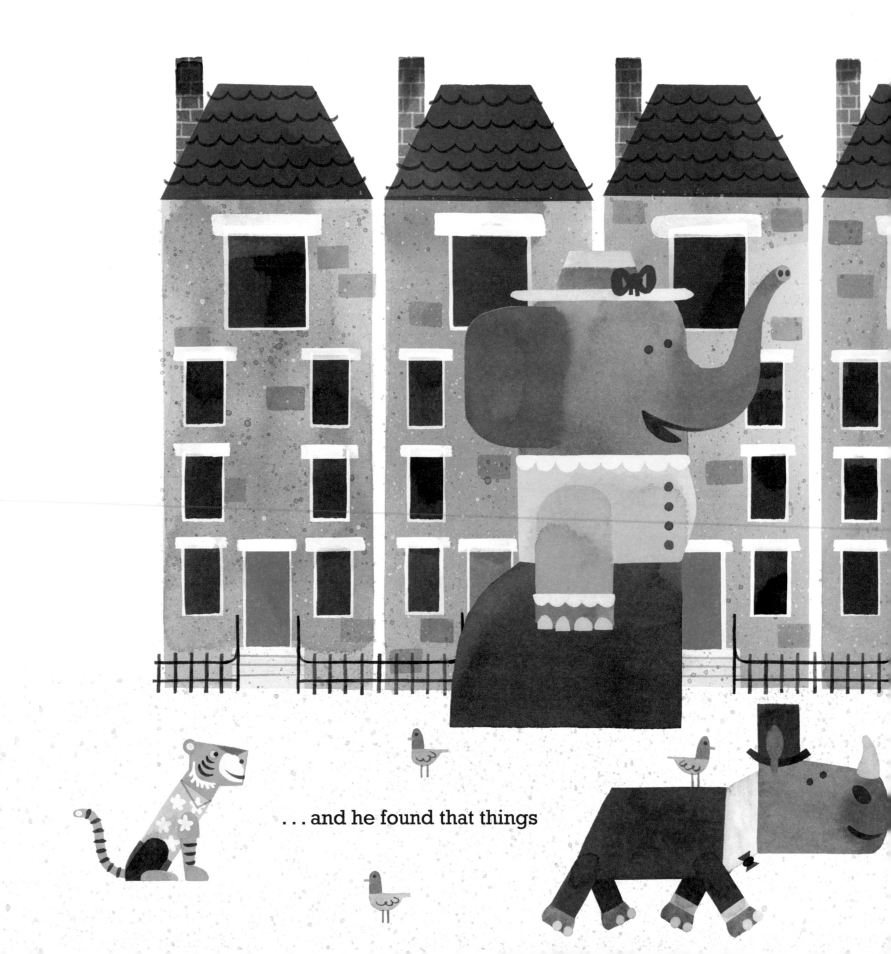

. . . and he found that things

were beginning to change.

Now Mr Tiger felt free to be himself.

And so did everyone else.

The End

About This Book

The illustrations for this book were made with India ink, watercolour, gouache, and pencil on paper, then digitally composited and coloured.

This book was edited by Alvina Ling and designed by Patti Ann Harris and Peter Brown. The original production was supervised by Jonathan Lopes and Charlotte Veaney, and the production editor was Barbara Bakowski.

The text was set in Rockwell, and the display type was hand-lettered by the author.